On Stage!

by Quinn Douglas
illustrated by Trevor Pye

Harcourt
SCHOOL PUBLISHERS

Printed in Mexico

ISBN 10: 0-15-351419-1
ISBN 13: 978-0-15-351419-7

Ordering Options
ISBN 10: 0-15-351212-1 (Grade 2 Advanced Collection)
ISBN 13: 978-0-15-351212-4 (Grade 2 Advanced Collection)
ISBN 10: 0-15-358054-2 (package of 5)
ISBN 13: 978-0-15-358054-3 (package of 5)

2 3 4 5 6 7 8 9 10   050   15 14 13 12 11 10 09 08 07

My name is Dion, and I'm in the second grade at Pitchford School. Three weeks ago, I was sitting at my desk listening to our teacher talk about the class play.

"Now, children, you all need to join in," I heard Ms. Lopez say. "The class play is a good way for you to show your talents. You can sing and dance, and play music."

I began to worry. I didn't want to sing, or dance, or play any music—not in front of an audience!

4

After school that day, Mom said,
"You look a little worried, Dion. Is
something the matter?"

I told my mom about the play,
and she understood my problem.
"Perhaps there is something else you
can do for the play," she said.
Then she asked the question,
"What's the play about?"

6

Mom listened as I told her the story. She laughed at the funny things that happen when a spaceship lands on earth.

"I have an idea," said Mom.
She led me to my room.

"Look at all your paintings," Mom
said, as she pointed to my walls. "You
can do something for the play! You're
good at painting, so maybe you can
paint the scenery."

8

I thought for a minute. Soon
I had a picture in my mind of what
I would do.

The next day, I couldn't wait to get to school to tell Ms. Lopez that I would like to draw and paint the scenery for the play.

"What a wonderful idea, Dion," she replied. "I'm sure that you will do a great job!"

Now here I am watching the play
from the side of the stage. I'm so
pleased with all the work that I've
done. Ms. Lopez bought me some
silver paint especially for painting
the spaceship. The stage looks great!

The play is awesome, and it's over
too quickly. As I walk away backstage,
I hear the audience clapping. Then
Ms. Lopez comes up to me and says,
"On stage, Dion!"

Now I feel shy again. I stand still for just a minute, but then I take a deep breath and follow Ms. Lopez onto the stage. She points to the scenery, and the audience claps and cheers loudly.

Suddenly, I am not shy anymore.
I bow and look down at Mom smiling
and clapping in the audience. I am
happy knowing that she is proud of
me. I feel proud, too.

14

Think Critically

1. What was Mom's solution when Dion was worried about being in the play?

2. How did Dion feel before and after he had spoken to Mom?

3. When Dion was on stage and Ms. Lopez pointed to the scenery, what did the audience do?

4. Why do you think the author wrote this story?

5. Do you think you would have enjoyed the play? Why or why not?

 Visual Arts

Draw Scenery The play at Dion's school was about space. Draw a picture showing what scenery you would make for a play about space.

 School-Home Connection Share *On Stage!* with a family member. Talk about things you are good at doing.

Word Count: 406